D1100097

C016752965

First published in 2019 in Great Britain by
Barrington Stoke Ltd
18 Walker Street, Edinburgh, EH3 7LP

www.barringtonstoke.co.uk

Text © 2019 Lisa Thompson
Illustrations © 2019 Mike Lowery

The moral right of Lisa Thompson and Mike Lowery to be
identified as the author and illustrator of this work has
been asserted in accordance with the Copyright,
Designs and Patents Act, 1988

A CIP catalogue record for this book is available
from the British Library upon request

ISBN: 978-1-78112-865-7

Printed in China by Leo

OWEN
AND THE
SOLDIER

LISA THOMPSON

With illustrations by
Mike Lowery

Barrington Stoke

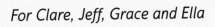

For Clare, Jeff, Grace and Ella

CHAPTER 1

Everyone has a secret, don't they? Not a big fat secret like they robbed a bank or they poisoned their grandma by accident. But small secrets. Something people keep hidden deep inside, hoping it won't bubble up their throat and burst out of their mouth for everyone to hear.

Maybe some people secretly wish they could be a stuntman in a Hollywood film or perhaps they secretly fancy Amelia Carey in class 9A. Or maybe their secret is something a bit ... different, like mine. Maybe they like to sit on a bench in the park and talk to a soldier. Not a living, breathing soldier, but a soldier made of stone.

There was a stone soldier in our park. The park wasn't really used any more, except as a shortcut on the way to somewhere else. There was an old toilet block that had bars on the window and was always locked, and there was a tennis court in the middle that was free to use. Someone stole the net last summer, so now it was just a rectangle of tarmac with a fence around it.

I walked across the park on my way to and from school. There was a war memorial garden behind some high hedges and I always looked in at the stone soldier inside. He sat on a bench, all on his own, and one day I saw he looked different. There was a white stain across the top of his cap. I thought someone had scribbled graffiti on the soldier at first, but when I got closer I realised it was bird poo. There was no one around, so I went in and over to the bench.

I got my drinking bottle out of my bag and dribbled some water on top of his head to wash the poo away. The water poured over his cap and ran down his face. I sat beside him on the bench.

"There's no need to cry about it," I said as I watched the water drip onto the dusty ground. "You can't sit there with poo on your head, can you? You'd look like a right idiot."

The stone soldier stared down at the floor. He wore a uniform from the First World War and sat leaning forward with his elbows on his knees.

I'd looked at the soldier many times as I walked past, but I'd never seen him close up before. There were a few lines across his forehead and his lips were pressed together. Some of his chin had crumbled away and half of one of his boots was missing. I thought he must have been sitting in the garden for a long time.

"Do you like being a soldier?" I asked him as I studied his face.

Dad once told me that in the last two years of the First World War, men didn't have a choice about fighting. The people in charge of the country made them go to war. I thought the stone soldier must have been one of those men. He didn't look so brave to me – he just looked like a normal man who was made to go to war.

"I don't think you do like it really, do you?" I said as I put my water bottle away and spotted a packet of tissues in the bottom of my bag. Mum had put them in there months ago. They were covered in tiny yellow ducks and far too embarrassing to use in school, but I kept forgetting to throw them away. I took a tissue out and began to wipe some of the water off the soldier's cheeks.

"Sorry about the ducks," I said.

I thought the soldier looked better now that he didn't seem like he was crying. I used another tissue to wipe the last of the poo from his head, then I got up and put them in a bin by the hedge.

The small area behind the hedge was known as the war memorial garden, but there weren't any flowers or plants in it. There was just the stone soldier on the bench, the bin and a plaque with twenty-five names engraved on it. Those were the names of men from our town who died during the First World War. I once asked Dad which one the soldier was, but Dad said that he represents all of the soldiers who died and that he wasn't a real-life person. I wanted to ask Dad what regiment he might have been in if he had been real. But I hadn't seen my dad for two years now, so that wasn't going to happen.

I sat back down on the bench and took out a tinfoil parcel. Inside was my leftover sandwich that I hadn't finished at lunch-time. I normally had ham and lettuce, but today I had fish paste because that was all I could find in the cupboard.

As I ate my sandwich, I watched the sun and shadows flicker across the soldier's back. I almost thought I'd see him move as he took a deep breath and sighed.

I screwed up the tinfoil and put it back into my bag and then I stood up.

"Well, I'll see you tomorrow then," I said, and I went out past the hedge.

And that was how it all started.

That was when I began to talk to the stone soldier.

CHAPTER 2

At school the next day, my first lesson was English, my worst subject. My English teacher was a man called Mr Jennings. He was young and funny and nice, but he was a big fan of something that he called "classroom participation". In fact, he liked it so much he had a poster on the wall behind his desk that said:

YOU ALL HAVE AN OPINION
LET'S HEAR IT!

All the teachers asked us questions in lessons, but Mr Jennings took it to another level. He asked questions *all* the time. Sometimes he even got us to stand up and shout out our favourite line from a book we were reading. Not all together, but everyone in turn. I hated his lessons because I hated talking in front of the class.

Today, Mr Jennings read a piece of poetry to us. Then he walked around the room, picked out people at random and asked them to talk about what they liked and didn't like about it.

"Kyle!" Mr Jennings said. "After hearing that poem, do you think Rupert Brooke was in favour of the war or against it?"

He asked questions in a nice way and he never got angry if someone said something really stupid. But he did get frustrated if you didn't say anything. Today, Mr Jennings pointed at me and asked, "Owen! What do you think Rupert Brooke meant when he used the words 'caught our youth'?"

I heard the entire class groan. All the other teachers knew I didn't like talking in class, so they didn't bother asking me questions any more. But Mr Jennings was quite new and he wouldn't give up.

I knew my answer, but I could still feel my face burning. The words jumbled around in my head. I tried to get my brain to grab hold of them and put them in the right order. I slowly opened my mouth. Mr Jennings folded his arms as he perched on the edge of his desk.

"Come on, Owen," Mr Jennings said. "You have views, I know you do. Share them with us!" He gave me a big grin.

I closed my mouth, looked down and shook my head. I heard Mr Jennings sigh.

"Unfortunately, it looks like Owen doesn't want to give us his opinion," he said. "Would anyone else like to share their views?"

I heard the rustle of school shirts as a few arms went up, and I relaxed a bit. Mr Jennings wouldn't waste time asking me any more questions today, so I was safe for now.

The last lesson was Geography. It was fine because we just watched a film about coastal erosion and then the bell went for the end of the day. I was the first person out of the door and heading home before the others had even pushed their chairs back in.

I walked down the road and turned into the park, making for the war memorial garden. I sat down next to the soldier, who didn't have any poo on him today. I took out my fish-paste sandwich and began to eat.

"Mr Jennings thinks he's an amazing teacher, but he isn't," I said to the soldier. "He thinks he's so cool and hip and different, but that's not teaching, is it? It's just pointless."

The stone soldier stared forward at the floor, listening.

"It wasn't that I didn't answer him because I didn't know what to say. I know exactly what 'caught our youth' meant in that poem."

I screwed up the tinfoil and threw it at the bin. I missed, so I picked it up from the floor, put it in the bin and sat back down.

"Rupert Brooke was happy about the war starting," I said. "That poem is all about how he and his friends were excited about going to war. The war 'caught' their youth. Do you get it?" I asked as I looked under the peak of the soldier's cap.

"I guess you didn't feel like that, did you?" I said. "I don't think you ever wanted to go to war. You were one of the men that was made to go."

I grabbed my water bottle from my bag and took a swig.

"It must have been really scary," I whispered. I scuffed my foot on the floor and then looked at my watch. It was nearly quarter to four. I didn't want to go home yet. I knew that Mum would be on the sofa when I got in, in her normal spot. She'd ask me how my day had been and I'd tell her that it had been the best. I would say that I'd told Mr Jennings what I thought about a poem that he'd read in class. Mum would smile at me, but her eyes would be as blank as the stone soldier's.

"Do you know what I want to be when I'm your age?" I said to the statue. "I want to be a stuntman."

It was true. Stuntmen got to be in all the best films and yet they didn't have to speak. *And* they were brave. I'd read up all about it and apparently you needed a wide range of skills. I was going to teach myself as many as I could.

"Do you know what I'm learning right now?" I said, and I tapped the soldier on the arm. "A forward roll. It might sound easy, but it's important to be able to do a perfect roll first. Then you can do more complicated moves like fight scenes and tumbling down the stairs. You need to be able to do a forward roll safely."

That was what the man on the YouTube video had said anyway.

"Do you want to see one?" I said.

I stood up and kicked a few stones out of the way.

"It's all about going over onto your shoulder," I explained. "Your head shouldn't touch the floor at all. Watch."

I crouched and placed one knee on the dry ground. I put my hands down, then tucked my head towards my left armpit and flipped over onto my right shoulder blade. I rolled along the length of my arm, then I sprang up onto my feet. It was just like the man's roll on the YouTube video. A small pebble had stuck to the palm of my hand and I picked it off as I stood up.

"See?" I said. "I bet you weren't expecting it to be so fast, were you? I've done about a hundred of those rolls and I think I'm nearly there. Then I'll move on to backward rolls and side rolls."

I dusted off my trousers and the back of my shirt. I didn't want to have to put them in the wash if I could help it. Mum got a bit stressed about that kind of thing now. I picked up my school bag and looked at the soldier. His sleeves were pulled up a bit and he looked strong, even though he wasn't big. I thought he'd have made a good stuntman too.

"I'll see you tomorrow then," I said. I patted the soldier on his cap, then turned away and headed home.

CHAPTER 3

I was late for school the next morning. I went to the office, as that was what you had to do when you were late. I told Mrs Bachman, the secretary, that my alarm hadn't gone off. She gave me a look. The kind of look someone gives you when they're figuring out whether what you said is true or not.

"That'll be a late mark for you on the register, Owen," Mrs Bachman said. "Are you sure it was to do with your alarm and nothing else?"

I looked down at the visitors' book on the desk in front of me, because I didn't want to look at Mrs Bachman any more.

"Yes, miss," I said. "It needed a new battery. I won't be late tomorrow."

Mrs Bachman tapped the desk with her pen.

"OK, well, get yourself to your first lesson then. You've only just missed registration."

I wasn't late because of my alarm clock. I was late because Mum was crying in the bathroom. I had to calm her down by sitting on the other side of the door and speaking to her. She came out eventually and said sorry to me and gave me a big hug. I told her to come downstairs and she sat on the sofa while I made her some toast and a cup of coffee. Then I rushed to get myself ready and ran to school. I didn't have time to say hello to the soldier.

My first lesson of the day was Art. It was my favourite class, so I hurried to get there as I didn't want to miss anything. We were making clay masks and I was really enjoying it. Our teacher, Miss Cannon, told us we could be as creative as we wanted. Even better, she let us get on with it and she wasn't interested in any "classroom participation" like Mr Jennings was.

I sat in my normal seat in the corner. Miss Cannon was walking around handing out our masks, which she'd wrapped in cling film so that they wouldn't dry out.

"Class 9A, I've been very impressed with your work so far," Miss Cannon said. "They're really coming together. Remember to put your hand up if you need any help."

She gave me a smile as she placed my mask onto my desk.

"Really good work, Owen," Miss Cannon told me. "I love the simplicity."

I smiled as I carefully unwrapped my mask. Most of the class were making African tribal masks or the kind that you'd wear at a masquerade ball. But mine was completely different. My mask was futuristic. I had smoothed out the clay and I'd made small rectangular holes for the eyes. I was going to make some flat shapes to look like nuts and bolts and then fix them on the sides of the forehead. I wanted it to look like a mask from a science-fiction film. When I became a stuntman, maybe I'd have to wear a mask like this if I was doing a fight sequence in space or something.

I was just making a square shape when I sensed someone standing beside my desk. I looked up. It was a girl called Megan who was in most of my classes.

"Can I borrow that smoothing thingy?" Megan said. I picked up the tool and passed it to her.

"You're really good, you know," she said as she stared at my mask. "Your mask is really original."

I nodded as I focused on what I was doing. Megan stood there for a few more seconds and then went back to her desk.

I used some water to stick my shapes on my mask and then I sat back. It was looking really good. Miss Cannon said we could paint the masks after they'd been fired. She might have thought I'd paint mine silver or gold or something metallic, but I was thinking of painting it entirely black and the shapes red. That would look really cool.

The lesson was over far too quickly – before I knew it we were packing up and getting ready for break.

"Before you go, 9A," Miss Cannon said, "can the following students head to classroom E10 before break-time?" She was reading from a slip of paper at the front of the class. "Those students are Megan, Sean and Owen."

I saw Megan and Sean look at each other, puzzled. What was all this about? I watched as they headed off out of the class. Then I slowly followed them to the English block, where E10 was. My stomach plummeted when I saw Mr Jennings standing in the doorway, waiting for us. He had a big grin on his face.

"Guys! Guys!" Mr Jennings said. "Thanks for coming down. Come in, come in." It was like he was welcoming us into his house. "Right, I wanted to talk to you all about the opening of the new library next week. We're having a ceremony and I would like you three to be involved."

Sean looked puzzled. "Doing what?" he said. Sean was clearly feeling as suspicious as I was.

"Poetry!" Mr Jennings said. He fanned out his hands like he was revealing something magical. "I want you three to each write a poem and read it out in front of the invited audience at the library opening."

Megan glanced at me. "All of us?" she said.

I knew what Megan was thinking. *Why have you picked Owen?* I was thinking the same thing myself.

"Yes, all of you!" Mr Jennings said. "You three have the best understanding of poetry in the class. I've read your essays and you're good."

"What's the poem got to be about?" Sean asked.

Mr Jennings glanced at his watch. I guessed it was time for his next class.

"Whatever you like," Mr Jennings said. "It doesn't have to be long, just a few lines each.

Perhaps pick your favourite thing to do and write about that?"

I opened my mouth to tell him that there was no way on earth I was going to stand up and read out a poem, but Mr Jennings left before I could speak.

Megan and Sean started talking about their poems before we'd even left the classroom. They didn't seem very happy about it, but they weren't questioning doing it.

"I suppose I could write something about running," Megan said. She had broken every track race record in the school. "What about you, Sean? What's your favourite thing?"

Sean shrugged and said, "I dunno. Gaming, I guess. But how can I write a poem about that?"

They both looked over at me.

"How about you, Owen?" Megan asked. "What are you going to write about?"

I picked up my bag.

"Nothing," I said. "I'm not doing it." And I headed outside for break.

CHAPTER 4

For the rest of the day I could sense Megan staring at me, but I avoided her eyes. I could tell that she was waiting for her moment to talk to me. After our last lesson had finished, I grabbed my stuff and was out of the door before anyone else. I jogged to the school gates, then headed to the park. I'd had an idea that I'd get Mum to write to the school, explaining that I wouldn't be there on the day of the library opening. She'd need to say I had a hospital appointment or something like that. But then I remembered you had to show a copy of a hospital letter if you had an appointment, and I didn't have a letter. I felt sick. There was no way I was going to read a poem out. Ever.

I got to the park and headed straight to the bench.

"Hi," I said to the soldier. I didn't fancy my sandwich today, so I just got it out of my bag and put it into the bin.

"You know that feeling when you get up in the morning and have a lot you're worrying about?" I asked the soldier. "But then something happens and you wish you could go back to that morning, because the worries you thought were bad weren't that bad after all?"

The soldier stared at the ground with his elbows fixed to his knees. I put my bag to one side and sat in exactly the same way. I focused on the ground and creased my forehead a bit, just like his. We sat there for a moment, our bodies mirroring each other.

"I don't want to do it, soldier," I said as I stared at the floor. "How can I get out of it? Mr Jennings won't take no for an answer." I looked across at the soldier in his uniform. He looked so anxious. His worries were far bigger than mine. I put my hand onto his cold arm and gave him a pat as I leaned back on the bench.

"Hey!" I said. "Do you want to see my vault? I've been practising it for when I'm a stuntman." I stood up. The breeze was getting up and a few leaves blew across the ground. "You do? Excellent! Well, like the forward roll, it sounds easy. But you need to learn how to do simple vaults before you get to try the harder ones."

I looked at the bench. I'd only tried a couple of vaults before and they were over a low wall in our back garden. The bench was much higher and wider.

"This one is all about putting your hands in the right place," I said, remembering what the man on YouTube had said. I walked behind the bench, as that was probably the easiest direction to jump from. Now I saw that the right side of the soldier's back was crumbling. It had a big hole in it as if he'd been shot. I didn't like it, so I looked away.

"Right. So you put your hands like this," I said, placing them on the bench. "And then you swing your feet over like this ..."

I got my left foot up onto the top, but as I brought my right foot around I caught it and toppled forwards. I crashed to the floor, my arms spread out in front of me. I felt my chin scrape against the hard ground.

I pushed myself up onto my knees. My shirt had ripped along one sleeve.

"Well, that wasn't supposed to happen," I said as I knelt there. I looked over at the soldier, who was staring right at me. The look on his face suddenly seemed really funny.

"There's no need to look so worried about it," I said to the soldier. "I haven't hurt myself." I looked at his crinkled forehead and then I started to laugh. It was one of those laughs that comes from nowhere, and before you know it you can't stop.

"I don't know ... what I was ... thinking," I said between gasps. "I've not tried to vault anything ... that high ... before!"

I laughed and clutched my stomach until it hurt. I took a few deep breaths, then stood up and inspected the rip in my shirt.

"I've only just started practising that one," I said to the soldier, breathing normally now. "Anyway, I'll see you tomorrow."

I picked up my bag and walked out of the memorial garden. I didn't have another clean shirt, so I'd have to put some washing on when I got home.

CHAPTER 5

The next morning I decided I was going to tell
Mr Jennings I wasn't going to read a poem.
After all, what could he do? He couldn't force
me to do it. I wasn't due to have English until
next week, but I wanted to get it over and done
with. I spotted Mr Jennings on break duty,
drinking a cup of coffee in the playground.

"Ah, Owen!" Mr Jennings said, beaming.
"How's the poem coming along?"

I stood in front of him but didn't look him in
the eye.

"I just wanted to tell you that I'm not doing it," I said.

Mr Jennings took a sip of his drink.

"I see," he said. "And why is that?"

I hadn't really thought about my answer. I couldn't say it was because I was scared, could I?

"I don't want to," I said.

We stood there in silence for a bit.

"I really think you should give it a go, Owen," Mr Jennings said. "I think your creative writing this term has been—"

"Look, I don't want to do it," I interrupted. "You can't make me, OK?" I stared him in the face this time.

Mr Jennings pursed his lips together and nodded.

"OK," he said. "I'll just leave it as Megan and Sean then. There's not time to get any other students involved now. Thanks for letting me know."

He turned away and walked towards a boy who had just dropped a wrapper on the ground.

I felt a bit sick, but I also felt a huge sense of relief. That had been a whole lot easier than I thought it would be.

After school, I headed straight to the memorial garden to tell the soldier.

"Mr Jennings didn't even really care!" I said as I sat beside him eating a bag of crisps. "I think he just picked me because he wanted to push me a bit. Some teachers are like that, you know. Sometimes they try and make you be someone you're not."

I ate the last of the crisp crumbs and put the bag in the bin.

"I don't think I'll be trying any vaults today," I said, smiling at the soldier. "I've got a big bruise on my knee from yesterday, see?"

I rolled up my trouser leg and pointed my knee at him, twisting it this way and that.

"I had to put my shirt in the bin too," I told the soldier. "I'm down to one school shirt now, so I'm going to have to—"

"Ah, there you are!" a voice said.

I let go of my trouser leg. Megan was walking into the garden.

"What are you doing here?" I said, scowling at her.

"I saw you come in here after school," Megan said. "How's your poem going? I've nearly finished mine."

I picked up my bag and swung it onto my shoulder, ready to leave.

"I'm not doing it," I said.

Megan frowned at me.

"Why?" she said.

I shrugged at her.

"I don't want to," I said. "I told Mr Jennings today and he's fine about it. It'll just be you and Sean."

Megan huffed and said, "That's not fair. But I guess Mr Jennings doesn't want to push you if you really don't want to."

We stared at each other and I felt myself blush.

Megan went over to the soldier. She put a hand on his arm and crouched down to get a better look at his face.

"He's so young," she said. "How old do you reckon he is?"

"I don't know. Twenty, maybe?" I said. It felt strange seeing someone else with him. It felt wrong.

Megan stood up again. "It's a shame the soldier's going, isn't it?" she said. "He's been here for as long as I can remember."

I froze.

"What?" I asked. "What do you mean he's going? Going where?"

Megan patted the soldier on the head, then looked straight at me.

"To be scrapped, I guess," she said. "The council are changing everything in the park. It was in the local paper weeks ago. My mum told me about it."

I blinked at her and then at the soldier.

"What? I don't understand," I said, my heart racing. "What do you mean they are changing everything?"

"They're going to rip everything out that's in here and redo it all," Megan told me. "The whole park is getting a revamp and they're starting with the war memorial garden. Didn't you know?"

I stared at her, my throat dry, and then I turned and ran home.

CHAPTER 6

When I got home, Mum was still in her pyjamas, watching TV on the sofa. I wasn't really in the mood to be all nice to her.

"Why haven't you got dressed, Mum?" I said from the doorway.

She turned to look at me and smiled.

"Owen!" Mum said. "You're home. Have you had a good day?"

I ignored her question and walked around the sofa and opened the curtains.

"It's really stuffy in here, Mum," I said. "Shall I open a window?"

Mum stared at the TV and didn't react.

"Mum, shall I open a window?" I said again.

She looked up at me. "Oh no, don't you worry about that," Mum said. "You go and do your homework."

She smiled, but her face dropped as soon as she looked back at the TV screen. The plate of toast I'd left for her this morning was still on the coffee table, untouched. I turned away and headed upstairs.

Mum hadn't always been like this. After Dad had gone, it had taken us a long time to adjust to being just the two of us, but we'd got there. Then, about a year ago, she'd begun to change. At first, she just seemed to forget to do stuff like brush her hair or make my packed lunch, but it got worse when she stopped

working. She was a photographer and she used
to be really busy with weddings and family
portraits, but then she stopped taking bookings.
Because she worked for herself, no one seemed
to notice. It wasn't like she went to an office
and didn't turn up one day. Then she stopped
changing out of her pyjamas and forgot to buy
food. Her friend Kate used to phone a lot and
turn up at our house, but Mum always managed
to smile and make an excuse. She'd say she
was just getting in the shower or she was going
out to do a photography job. But as soon as
Mum closed the door or put the phone down,
she'd just head back to the sofa.

Kate texted me once. She said:

**Owen. Is everything OK? I haven't
heard from your mum in a while. Do
ring me if you need me, won't you?
Kate x**

I replied and told Kate that everything was fine.
I said that Mum was busy with work and she'd

be in touch. Kate didn't reply, but I kept her message on my phone.

After I'd left Mum staring at the TV, I went to my room and switched on my laptop. I wanted to find out what was going on with the soldier in the memorial garden. The first page that came up was an article from the local newspaper. It was dated four months ago.

Town Memorial Soldier Being Scrapped

He might have sat on the bench for the past fifty years, but the town's memorial soldier has now served his time and is destined for the bin. Council member Camilla Broadly said the council have exciting plans to revamp the memorial garden:

"There is no doubt that the stone soldier has done the town proud," Camilla told us. "But he's clearly seen better days and is beginning

to crumble. Once we have removed the soldier, we will create a peaceful area with flowerbeds, a cross and a new bench. The plaque displaying the names of those who died in the war will remain."

I couldn't believe it. Megan was right. They were scrapping the soldier! Why? OK, so he was a bit crumbly in places, but surely not so bad that they had to put him in the bin?

Underneath the article, there was a small drawing of how the garden would look after the work. There was a bench, two flowerbeds, a tall stone cross and the plaque with the names. It looked empty without the soldier. Lower down, there was a line with an email address:

What do you think about the council's plans? Send an email to our Features Editor at the following address ...

I thought for a moment. The article was old, but the work hadn't happened yet, so surely something could be done? I opened up my email account and began to type.

Dear Features Editor,

I am writing to you about the removal of the First World War soldier from the town's memorial garden. I don't believe that this should happen. My dad said that the soldier represents all those who died in the war. I think taking him away would be wrong.

Yours sincerely,
Owen Fletcher

I hit *send* before I had a chance to think about it. There, it was done now. I'd never emailed a newspaper before. Then I searched for the local council's website. There was a long list of all the departments and I clicked on "Planning", hoping it was the right one. There was an email address for enquiries to the planning office, so I copied my message to the newspaper and sent it to them. Then I turned my laptop off and went downstairs to find something for dinner.

CHAPTER 7

The next day, I left for school a few minutes
earlier than normal. I wanted to check in on
the soldier and make sure there were no signs
that work would be starting soon.

When I went into the memorial garden,
I saw that someone had put an empty can of
Coke on the soldier's knee and wrapped a dirty
old tea towel around his head. It made me feel
a bit sick to see him looking like that.

"It could have been worse, I suppose," I said
as I took the towel off his head and put it and

the Coke can in the bin. "At least it isn't bird poo."

I sat down beside the soldier. I could hear a blackbird singing in a tree behind us and the distant sound of a bus going along the High Street.

"I've got something to tell you," I said to the soldier. I could feel a painful lump forming in my throat. "The council said they are going to do up the memorial garden. They want to make a lot of ... changes."

I looked at the soldier's cold, anxious face and I swallowed.

"But it's going to be OK," I said, trying to sound cheerful. "I've sent the newspaper an email and I've sent one to the council too. I'm going to get them to change their mind."

I put my hand on the soldier's rough arm and rubbed his sleeve. Some of the stone crumbled against my fingers. I could see he was damaged, but surely there must be a way to repair him rather than get rid of him altogether?

"The council don't understand how important you are, that's the problem," I said. "And if they can't see it, then I'll have to—"

"Oh, hello again," a voice said.

I took my arm away fast and flicked my head round. It was Megan. She was standing by the entrance in her school uniform. She opened her mouth to say something but shut it again. She'd definitely heard me talking.

I picked up my bag, put my head down and stumbled past her. I could feel my cheeks burning. If Megan told anyone that I'd been talking to a statue, no one at school would let me forget it.

"Hey, wait up," Megan said, catching up to me. "I thought we could walk to school together. I normally go down the High Street, but I thought I'd come by the park for a change."

I ignored her and kept walking.

"Do you go to see the soldier every day?" Megan asked.

"What's it to you?" I snapped back as I walked faster. My face was still burning.

Megan dropped back for a moment, then caught me up again. "My mum said they'll be starting work on the garden any time now," she said.

I stopped.

"Already? B-but how!" I stuttered. "How can you know that? They can't take the soldier away. It's wrong!"

Megan's bottom lip stuck out.

"My mum works for the council," she replied. "She doesn't work in that department, but she knows all about it because she's involved with the money and budgets and stuff."

"Can you tell her to tell them not to do it?" I said.

Megan shrugged. "I dunno. I don't think it'll make much difference. The decision has been made. He's crumbling away, Owen. The soldier can't really stay like that, can he?"

I shook my head.

"You're wrong," I said. "He's fine. He just needs repairing, that's all. You should tell your mum they're wasting money, that's what they're doing! It would be cheaper to fix him than do all of that work, surely?"

We began to walk again.

"I would have thought they'd have looked into that, wouldn't you?" Megan said. "I know the council are always trying to save money."

She stopped and put her hand on my arm.

"Sorry, Owen. I can understand why he means so much to you, especially after ..."

I shrugged her hand off.

"You don't understand anything!" I shouted.

I turned away and walked quickly towards school. And this time Megan didn't catch me up.

CHAPTER 8

I spent all that day thinking about how I was going to save the soldier. I hoped that once the newspaper got interested, they'd start writing stories about it. Then surely other people would get involved and there'd be some kind of protest? That was what this needed – other people. I couldn't save the soldier all on my own.

I didn't go to see him on my way home after school. I wanted to get home as soon as possible to see if anyone at the newspaper or the council had answered my emails.

When I got in, Mum was in the kitchen peeling some potatoes. She was dressed as well, which meant it was a good day.

"Hi, Mum," I said.

"Oh, hello, darling," she answered. "How was school?"

"Fine," I said, sitting down on a kitchen chair.

Mum dropped a curl of potato peel onto the counter.

"I was thinking of making some chips for tea. I've just looked and we haven't got much in the fridge, I'm afraid."

I knew this already. I'd planned to go and get a few things from the local shop a bit later.

"Chips sound great," I said. "I can get some fish fingers if you like?"

Mum smiled at me, her eyes looking watery.

"That's a lovely idea, thank you," she said.

She put the peeler down.

"I'm sorry I'm not myself at the moment, Owen," Mum said. "I will get there, I promise you. Ever since your dad—"

"Don't worry, Mum," I said, interrupting her and getting up. "I've just got to do something and then I'll pop to the shop."

I left the kitchen before she could say any more.

When I checked my emails, I had two messages. One was from the planning office at the council. I opened it right away.

Dear Owen,

Thank you very much for your email.

I am sorry to hear you are disappointed that the stone soldier in the war memorial garden is due for removal. If you have visited the garden recently, I'm sure that you will appreciate that the statue is in a very poor condition and not a fitting tribute to the bravery of our fallen soldiers. However, I am thrilled to let you know that work on a new garden will be commencing very soon!

After the garden has been completed, I would be interested to hear your views. I'm sure you will like it!

With kind regards,
Camilla Broadly

My heart was pounding. Not a fitting tribute? How could she say that! Of course the soldier was a fitting tribute! He represented so much. I clicked on the other email. It was from the local newspaper.

Dear Owen,

Thank you for your email. I agree. It's very sad that the soldier is being removed from the memorial garden, but I'm afraid this is rather old news now. I believe that work will be starting very soon, so there isn't much time left to try to change the council's plans.

All the best,
Guy Evans
Features Editor

This was awful. If the newspaper wasn't interested, then who would be? I turned the laptop off and went back downstairs.

Mum gave me some money and I headed to the corner shop to get the fish fingers for tea.

The fish fingers were in the freezer at the back of the shop. I picked up a box of them and a bag of frozen peas. I went to the counter and put them down next to a pile of newspapers. The lady on the till kept looking at me.

"You're from that school with the new library, aren't you?" she said, and nodded at my school tie.

I nodded.

"They're making a right fuss about it in the paper, you know," the till lady said. "There aren't many schools getting libraries put in nowadays, you know. They're too busy ripping them out."

She rang up my items on the till.

"It's even made the front page," she said as she tapped at the newspaper on top of the pile.

I glanced at the small article in the corner of the front cover.

Mayor To Open School Library

The Mayor will be joining council members and students and staff of Charrington High to open their new school library on Monday. Councillor Camilla Broadly said, "It's always a thrill to see a library open in a school and I'll be honoured to attend the ceremony ..."

I picked up my things and left the shop. As I walked home, my mind raced. The council woman was going to be at the opening ceremony on Monday and I could be there too. *If* I read out a poem. Maybe I could do it? Maybe I could change Camilla Broadly's mind about the soldier?

CHAPTER 9

On Monday morning I woke up exhausted. I'd
been up until midnight trying to finish my
poem. I'd been trying to write it all weekend
and I still wasn't completely happy with it, but
it would just have to do. I folded up the piece
of paper, put it in my bag and said goodbye to
Mum.

When I walked into the park, I saw a truck
parked on the grass beside the memorial
garden. A couple of men were getting mesh
fences off the back of the truck and piling
them onto the ground. It looked like they were
planning to fence off the area, ready to do some

work. The men stood around for a bit, talking about something, then they both climbed back in the truck and drove off. I ran over to the hedge entrance, tears prickling my eyes. The soldier was still there. There was still hope.

I got to school earlier than I needed to, because I had to find Mr Jennings and tell him that I'd changed my mind about reading a poem. I found him in the library, setting out the chairs ready for the ceremony. It was the first time I'd seen the new library completely finished. It was bright and light and smelled of fresh paint and new books. It looked amazing.

Mr Jennings was shocked when I told him, but he said that I could read my poem after Megan. He put his hand on my arm and gave it a squeeze.

"Well done, Owen," he said. "I know things have been tough for you, what with your dad and everything. I'm really looking forward to hearing the poem."

I nodded back at him, then went off to my first lesson.

The ceremony began at 2 p.m. Megan, Sean and I had to make our way to the library at 1.30 to get ready. I felt sick with nerves. Even Megan looked scared and she couldn't stop talking.

"What's your poem about, Owen?" Megan asked me. "Mine is about running and how it feels to be racing against other people. What about yours, Sean? Did you write about gaming in the end? I hope we get a microphone. Do you think we'll get a microphone?" She didn't give us a chance to answer any of her questions, so I didn't try.

When we got to the library, some of the guests were already arriving and taking their seats. The front row of chairs had pieces of paper on them saying "Reserved" and the person's name was written underneath. I spotted that Camilla Broadly, the councillor, was sitting right in the centre.

"Ah! Wonderful. You all ready?" Mr Jennings asked, coming over to me, Megan and Sean. He directed us to three seats to one side. There was a lectern with a microphone in the middle, where we'd stand and read our poems. I felt my legs begin to tremble.

"The head teacher is going to give a speech at the start and do all the thank-yous," Mr Jennings said. "Then I'll be talking for about five minutes about reading and books and all that jazz ..."

He waved his hands at us like he was going to do a dance, and Sean snorted.

"Then, Sean, it's over to you for your poem," Mr Jennings went on. "Please each begin by saying what the poem is about briefly before you read it out loud. Megan, you'll be on next, then, Owen, you'll finish things off. OK, everyone?" Mr Jennings gave us a big grin and dashed off to rearrange one of the book displays that had toppled over.

The three of us sat on our seats and Megan jiggled her knees up and down. The library was only small and a few invited students began to take their seats at the back.

My heart was pounding so hard it felt like it was going to burst out of my chest. I wondered if I could get Mr Jennings' attention and tell him I couldn't do it after all.

"Are you OK, Owen?" Megan asked. "You look really flushed."

I swallowed. My throat felt so dry.

"I can't do it," I said, shaking my head at her.

Megan frowned at me. "Of course you can. If you don't feel brave, just pretend to be. That's what I do."

I swallowed again. My throat felt sore, like I needed a drink. I closed my eyes and focused on my breathing. When I opened my eyes, the front row was full. Camilla Broadly was sitting in her seat, smiling to a man beside her. She looked nice. She had kind eyes.

"What's your poem about, Owen?" Sean asked me as he leaned around Megan.

I opened my mouth to answer, but the head teacher tapped on the microphone.

"Welcome, everybody!" she said. "I'm so pleased to see you all here on this very special day ..."

The head teacher went on to talk about how proud she was to have such a fantastic library in her school.

My hands began to shake. Was I putting myself through this for nothing? Was it all going to be too little, too late? The workmen were clearly going to be starting the work today. Was the soldier already in pieces? I felt tears tickle my eyes. I couldn't cry, not here in front of all these people.

The audience gave a polite clap as Mr Jennings stood in front of the lectern. He started talking about the importance of stories in everyone's lives. Sean got his poem out of his pocket and unfolded it, ready. I could see it was only a few lines.

Soon Mr Jennings had finished his speech and was asking the audience to give Sean a big round of applause. Sean got up and headed towards the microphone.

"Hello," Sean said quietly. "My poem is about gaming, because I like playing computer games."

Mr Jennings made a groaning noise and the audience laughed. And then Sean began to read:

I choose my weapons,
By hitting the X button …

Sean's poem was good. It didn't rhyme and it wasn't very long, but everyone was smiling and they gave him a nice clap. Sean folded the poem up and walked back to his seat. Mr Jennings asked the audience to welcome Megan, then she got up to read hers.

"My name is Megan and I like running," she began. "My poem is all about how it feels to win a race." She looked down at her piece of paper and read:

The starting gun fires,
I shoot off down the track,
I race round the corner,
They're chasing my back …

Megan read her poem so well that every person in the audience was perched on the edge of their seat. When she got to the end and described crossing the finishing line in a blaze of glory, the whole crowd cheered and clapped. Megan came back to her seat, grinning away.

Then Mr Jennings announced my name. The audience clapped, but I couldn't move. I was frozen to my seat.

Megan gave me a nudge. "It's fine," she whispered. "Just pretend, OK? Just pretend to be brave."

I looked back at her and thought of the soldier on the bench. I thought about how brave he was. And then I stood up slowly to take my turn.

CHAPTER 10

My legs shook all the way to the lectern and I gripped hold of it when I got there. Mr Jennings gave me a thumbs-up and a big grin. Camilla Broadly from the council gave me a nice smile and I cleared my throat and began to speak.

"My name is Owen Fletcher," I said. "And I ... I ..."

I stopped and looked up at everyone, and then my throat closed up. I opened my mouth, but nothing came out. I could feel my face start to burn. I looked over at Mr Jennings, and he had a worried look on his face. A few people gazed down at their hands and someone at the back coughed. I swallowed, then swallowed again. I couldn't do it. I shut my eyes and took a deep breath, and then I opened my eyes again.

"My name is Owen Fletcher," I began. I looked right at Camilla Broadly as I spoke, and she blinked back at me. I wondered if she recognised my name from my email.

"My poem is about my dad," I said. "And I'd like to dedicate it to the stone soldier who sits in the memorial garden."

The library went absolutely silent. I unfolded my piece of paper and placed it on the lectern. This was it. This was my moment to save him. I cleared my throat and then I read:

Something Simple
by Owen Fletcher

Something simple,
Can remind me of you.
A mug in a cupboard.
A stranger in blue.

An old stone soldier,
Making me smile.
He's crumbling now,
He's been there for a while.

My dad went to war
But he didn't come home.
He won't hear me laugh,
Like the soldier of stone.

One is now gone,
But the other must stay.
Save the stone soldier,
Don't take him away.

That was it. I'd finished, but the library was still completely silent. Not one person clapped. I kept my head down and folded my sheet of paper. I couldn't believe it. It was a disaster. They hated it.

I took a deep breath, then looked up at the room. Suddenly there was applause like thunder. My jaw dropped open. Everyone was grinning at me and clapping madly. Some people even started standing up. Camilla Broadly dabbed a tissue at the corner of her eye as she fumbled in her bag for something. She pulled out her phone, swiped the screen, then walked out of the library with it pressed to her ear.

Mr Jennings came over and patted me on the back.

"Thank you, Owen," he said, his eyes glistening. "That was really ... brilliant."

I smiled and sat down with Megan and Sean, who were both still clapping like crazy.

I sat back. That was it. That was all I could do.

CHAPTER 11

As I was walking home afterwards, Megan came up to me.

"I thought what you did was really brave," Megan said. "Your poem was brilliant."

I nodded and smiled. I was so tired. When I got home, I'd have to go out again and get something for dinner. I was sure Mum wouldn't have thought of it.

Megan stopped as we got to the park.

"I'm sorry about your dad, Owen," she said. "It must have been really difficult for you and your mum."

"Thanks, Megan," I said.

The whole school knew about my dad, but no one ever talked to me about it. My dad had been in the army and he'd gone to Syria two years ago. Just like those soldiers whose names were on the plaque in the memorial garden, my dad never came back.

"I'll see you tomorrow," Megan said. Then she headed down the High Street as I crossed over to the park.

The metal fences that the men had taken off the truck this morning were now surrounding the hedge around the memorial garden. I rushed over to the entrance. The soldier was still there. They hadn't started work yet. I walked along the fence until I found a small gap and I squeezed myself in.

I went up to the soldier and sat down beside him. His elbows rested on his knees as he gazed at the ground. I placed my hand on his arm. It felt cold and rough. I looked under his cap into his sad eyes.

"I don't think you should be scared any more," I said. I rested my head against the soldier's arm as tears began to fall down my face.

"I'll never forget you, I promise," I told the soldier. "I'll always remember you, OK?"

I closed my eyes and cried until I didn't have any tears left. I wiped my face, then wiped the soldier's cheek with my wet hand. I stood up, kissed the top of his head and then turned away and walked home.

CHAPTER 12

Mum stayed in bed the next morning. Normally she'd get up for a cup of tea before I went to school, but today it looked like she really couldn't manage it. I went into her room.

"I'll see you later, Mum," I said as I put a mug of tea on her bedside table. I saw that Dad's sweater was lying on the duvet beside her.

"Thank you, Owen," Mum said, her voice muffled. "Have a nice day."

On my way across the park, I could see that they were starting work early on the memorial garden. A man in an orange jacket was walking around and talking on his phone. One of the metal fences had been removed, so I could get to the entrance to the garden. I walked over and looked in at the bench when the man had his back turned.

My heart tightened.

The bench was empty.

The soldier was gone.

CHAPTER 13

The first lesson at school that day was English. Mr Jennings asked Megan and Sean to read their poems out again so that everyone could hear them. He asked me quietly if I wanted to read mine as well, but I said no. This time Mr Jennings just nodded and said that was fine.

The rest of the day was a haze. I kept thinking about the soldier and whether they'd broken him up into bits yet. Megan kept looking over at me, her face all concerned. She tried to talk to me at lunch-time, but I walked away. I didn't want to talk to anyone – not today.

I ran across the park after school. The workers were there, smashing up the concrete paving and chucking great slabs into the back of a truck. I didn't want to look in case I saw the soldier in pieces.

When I got home, Mum was still in bed. I went up and saw the tea I'd left for her that morning still on the bedside table, stone cold. I didn't say anything. I didn't want to get anything from the shop tonight. I'd just have some toast.

I put my laptop on and sat on my bed, staring at my carpet. I suddenly felt so, so lonely. Dad had gone, the soldier had gone and now I was losing Mum.

My laptop made a "ding", telling me that an email had arrived. I looked in my inbox and saw there was an email from Camilla Broadly. I quickly clicked on it and read:

Dear Owen,

I had to write to you after hearing you read your incredibly moving poem at your school yesterday. You are a very brave person indeed, Owen. I'm sure your father would be very proud.

I have had a chat with my colleagues here and we have decided to make a few changes to our memorial garden plans. I will be in touch with you again soon.

Yours sincerely,
Camilla Broadly

Changes? What did she mean by changes? My stomach turned over with excitement, but I couldn't escape the fact that the soldier was gone, however hopeful I felt. I'd tried to save him and I'd lost.

I thought of Mum, lying in bed in the room next to me. I was losing her too.

I took my phone out of my bag and scrolled down my texts until I found the one from Mum's friend Kate. I pressed reply and began to type:

Hi Kate, it's Owen. I think I need your help.

CHAPTER 14

A few weeks later, an envelope came through our door addressed to Master Owen Fletcher.

Inside was an invitation for me and Mum to attend the grand opening of the new memorial garden that weekend. Camilla Broadly had added in a hand-written note that said: "I hope to see you there, Owen. Camilla."

On the morning of the opening, Kate came over to see how we were doing. After I'd sent my text to her, she'd started coming round most days and she had taken Mum to see the doctor. Mum wasn't close to being her old self again, but she was getting there.

I put a shirt on with my jeans, and Mum wore a green dress that I hadn't seen her wear for years.

"You both look amazing," said Kate. "Now, go and enjoy yourselves and I'll get us some lunch sorted, OK?"

Mum pressed her lips together and touched Kate's arm.

"Thank you," Mum said.

When we walked to the park, Mum put her arm through mine. Normally I would have hated her doing that in public, but today I didn't mind.

"I'm excited to see what they've done, aren't you?" Mum said.

I nodded. I was excited but also very nervous.

A small crowd had gathered at the front of the hedge and a bright red ribbon was tied across the entrance. I tried to get a look in, but there were too many people in the way. Five old men wearing army uniforms were near the front. One of them had so many medals on his chest there was barely room for them all.

Camilla spotted me and came over. She was wearing a bright purple dress and she looked a bit like she was going to a wedding.

"Owen!" Camilla said. "I'm so pleased to see you! And you must be Mrs Fletcher." She shook Mum's hand. "I'm Camilla from the local council. I must say, you have one incredible son there."

Mum smiled and blushed a bit.

"I know," Mum said. "He's everything to me."

"What happened to the soldier?" I asked.

Camilla was about to answer when someone came over and tapped her on the arm, saying the ceremony was about to begin. I tried again to see around the crowd into the garden, but there were still too many people.

"Thank you all for coming ..." Camilla said, now standing by the entrance. She began by talking about the local soldiers who had served in the war. She read the list of names that I remembered from the plaque behind the bench, then said a prayer. Camilla asked one of the old soldiers to cut the ribbon and declare the garden open. The soldier with all the medals stepped forward and stood by the ribbon with a pair of shiny silver scissors.

"It gives me great pleasure to declare the new memorial garden open," the old soldier said, and he snipped the ribbon. Everyone clapped and then people began to drift in to take a look.

Mum stepped forward, but I was frozen to the spot. I couldn't move.

"Aren't you going to have a look?" Mum asked.

"You go first," I said. "I'll wait until it's not so busy."

Mum moved with the crowd towards the garden and I could hear people chatting happily from behind the hedge. I swallowed as Camilla looked at me. She nodded to me, but she didn't come over.

I stood there for a few minutes and then people started making their way out of the garden with smiles on their faces. I walked a bit closer to the entrance. There were only a few people in there now, including my mum.

My stomach flipped over as I walked slowly into the garden.

I looked to the right where the soldier had sat, but a new raised flowerbed was in his place. It was planted with a few rose bushes and I saw a white butterfly flitter between the flowers. Straight ahead of me was a brand-new bench. Mum was sitting with her face turned to the sun. Beside her was a figure, leaning forward with his elbows on his knees. It was the stone soldier. He was back!

I went over to the bench and Mum opened her eyes.

"Oh, Owen," she said. "Isn't it lovely in here? So peaceful. I should come here more often, you know. It's a nice place to be."

I sat down beside the stone soldier. He had been repaired, his chin had been rebuilt and his foot was complete. I looked behind him and saw that the hole in his back had been filled. I smiled.

"We could come here together, if you like?" I said, looking across at Mum. "You could bring your camera and take a few photos."

She turned and smiled at me.

"That'd be nice," Mum said, and she closed her eyes again as the sun shone on her face.

I looked under the soldier's cap as he stared down towards the ground. His face didn't look as anxious now. There were creases in the corners of his mouth. Just tiny ones, but they made his face look more relaxed than it had before.

I let out a deep sigh.

"Hello, soldier," I whispered, and I patted him on the arm.